Contents

Acknowledgment: Rebecca Archer for the front cover illustration.

Ladybird books are widely available, but in case of
difficulty may be ordered by post or telephone from:

Ladybird Books – Cash Sales Department
Littlegate Road Paignton Devon TQ3 3BE
Telephone 0803 554761

A catalogue record for this book is available
from the British Library

Published by Ladybird Books Ltd Loughborough Leicestershire UK
Ladybird Books Inc Auburn Maine 04210 USA

bedtime
stories for
under fives

by JOAN STIMSON

illustrated by
GRAHAM ROUND

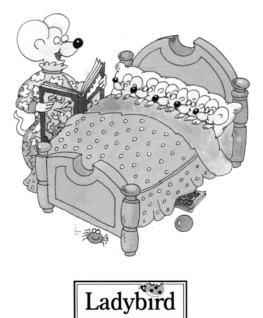

Ladybird

The runaway mouse

"I'm just popping out for some supper," said Mrs Mouse.

And a few minutes later she staggered back with a huge hunk of cheese.

"Ooooh!" squeaked five small voices. "Can we have some now, Mum?"

"No, you can't," said Mrs Mouse. "This cheese is for supper."

But the smallest mouse couldn't wait.

"Mmmm!" The cheese tasted
WONDERFUL… until Mum caught her.

"BED!" cried Mrs Mouse. "And no more
cheese for a week!"

The little mouse felt so sorry for herself that
she bolted right out of the family hole into the
big wide farmyard.

"Watch out!" snapped a cross voice. It belonged to a puppy.

"I'm running away," the little mouse told him. "Mum shouted. She said I couldn't have any more cheese."

"But did she stop you playing football?" asked the puppy.

The little mouse looked surprised and shook her head.

"Well, think yourself lucky. Mine did. And just because I was a bit rough. Would YOU like to be goalkeeper?"

The little mouse took one look at the tangle of puppies on the lawn and carried on running. She ran so fast that she almost fell into the duck pond.

"Going for a swim?" quacked a glum voice.

The little mouse shook her head.

"Nor me," said the duckling. "I'm not allowed in today. And just because I was a bit cheeky. But I could teach YOU how to dive."

The little mouse shivered as the other ducklings swam by. Then she carried on running.

"Not so fast!" hissed a black and white calf.

"I can't stop!" squeaked the little mouse.
"I'm running away. Because Mum shouted."

"I wish I could shout!" hissed the calf.
"I MOOED a bit too loudly last night. And
now I'm only allowed to *whisper*!"

"WOW! Was that noise ALL YOU?" cried
the little mouse. "You woke everyone up and
frightened us. Mum had to bring us a
midnight feast and tell us another…"

"WHOOSH!" Suddenly the little mouse felt so homesick that she ran all the way back to her hole. She dived straight into bed with her brothers and sisters and was just in time for a… STORY!

Cock a doodle help!

Cock a doodle do!
We don't know what to do.
Our rooster's lost his sense of time
And shouts at half-past two!

Cock a doodle pain!
…there he goes again.
Granny's packed her bags and gone,
She caught the early train!

Cock a doodle Dad!
My dad is hopping mad.
If Rooster went away as well,
I know that he'd be glad!

Cock a doodle Vet!
Please help us with our pet.
Check out his pulse and test his clock
(But don't make him upset!)

Cock a doodle hey!
He crowed at DAWN today.
He's back to normal, thank you, Vet,
Your skill has made our day!

Cat's cradle

Dad was taking Ben to choose a kitten.

The kittens had been born on a houseboat.
And their owner wanted to find homes for
them... before they jumped overboard!

Ben pointed to a handful of white fluff with a
black patch.

"That one," he said. "And I'll call him Pirate."

Pirate liked living with Ben. But he didn't like
his basket.

Pirate spent hours clawing the cushion and twisting this way and that. His expression grew more sour by the minute.

"Perhaps Pirate's cold," said Ben. He opened the airing cupboard door and lifted the kitten inside.

Pirate poked about among the clean washing. Then he arched his back and gave a loud sniff of disgust.

"Perhaps Pirate's missing his mum," said Dad.

So he got out Ben's old carrycot. Dad surrounded Pirate with baby blankets and gave him a big blue rabbit.

"WHOOOSH!" Pirate shot out of the carry-cot. And GLARED over his shoulder.

Pirate couldn't stand the sofa. He thought the beds were a dead loss.

And, although he snatched the odd catnap, Pirate never had a really good sleep.

Then one day Pirate went missing.

Ben and Dad searched the house from top to bottom. Next they tried the garden.

"Whatever's that noise?" said Dad. He looked across at the washing line.

"IT'S PIRATE!" cried Ben. "He's been asleep in the peg bag and he's PURRING!"

Dad watched Pirate swinging gently in the breeze.

"Of course," he said. "I should have known. Pirate is missing the feel of the water."

That evening Dad made a pint-sized hammock. He slung it between the beams in Ben's room.

"What do you think, Pirate?" asked Ben.

Pirate didn't claw or sniff or glare or disappear.

He just climbed into his hammock. And went to bed happily ever after!

Is Mr Marshall
a Martian?

It was too hot to sleep. It was too hot even to read her new space book. So Lucy knelt down and gazed out of the window.

Next door Mrs Marshall was still gardening. At last she stretched and put away her rake. Lucy was just beginning to feel drowsy, when something else caught her eye.

It was a shadowy figure in the Marshalls' garden. And she was sure the figure was wearing a space helmet!

Lucy shot back into bed. Her book lay open on the pillow.

"IS THERE LIFE ON MARS?" it said.

Lucy slammed the book shut and pulled up the sheet.

For the next few evenings Lucy looked out at the Marshalls' garden… from behind her curtains.

But all she saw was Mrs Marshall weeding and Mr Marshall cutting the grass.

"I must have dreamt it," said Lucy.

But Lucy spoke too soon. There it was again…
the same shadowy figure and the same space
helmet!

Lucy fumbled under the bed for her
telescope. But the figure had disappeared into
the bushes. And all Lucy could see was a pair
of boots… big silver boots which sparkled in
the evening sunlight.

Lucy lay on her bed and thought what to do next.

Before she could decide, there was a ring at the door.

DING-A-LING-LING!

"I've come to borrow some cable."

It was Mr Marshall, talking to Dad. Lucy dashed downstairs. She would tell them both at once. After all, it was only fair to warn the Marshalls.

Lucy burst into the living room.

"Whatever is it?" asked Dad.

But Lucy only gasped… because Mr Marshall was wearing boots… big silver boots which glinted against the dark carpet!

Lucy fled back upstairs.

"Is Mr Marshall a Martian?" she asked herself over and over again.

Then there were other, more confusing, questions.

"Why doesn't Mr Marshall wear his space helmet ALL the time? And where does he keep his spaceship?

"Oh no!" groaned Lucy suddenly. "His spaceship must be broken. And I bet it needs some NEW CABLE!"

Lucy fell into a troubled sleep before Dad could tuck her in. She woke late and anxious next morning.

DING-A-LING-LING! Dad went to answer the door.

Lucy crept out of bed and peered through the banisters.

Mr Marshall looked pleased with himself. He handed Dad a jar with a homemade label.

"MARSHALL'S PRIZE HONEY," it said, and there was a picture of a huge bee.

"Good heavens!" cried Dad. "Don't you worry about getting stung?"

"Not with my special beekeeping helmet and boots," said Mr Marshall. "They work a treat... even if they do make me look like someone from outer space!"

All day long Lucy felt rather silly. That evening she tried to spot Mr Marshall's beehives from her window. The Marshalls looked up from their garden and waved.

When Dad came to tuck in Lucy, he was holding an invitation.

"Tom's having a fancy dress party," he said. "But we don't have anything for you to wear."

"Mr Marshall does," cried Lucy brightly. "I'll ask if I can borrow his beekeeping helmet and boots. And I'll go as a MARTIAN!"

Jake and the jumble panic

"Where's Wilfred?" shouted Jake at bedtime.

Wilfred was a battered bear with blue trousers. And Jake's oldest possession.

"You'll have to wait a minute," Mum shouted back. She sipped her coffee slowly. "I never knew sorting out jumble could be so exhausting."

All of a sudden Jake had that sinking feeling.
HE'D sorted out a big bag of jumble, too.
And Wilfred had been 'helping'.

What if Wilfred had got mixed up with the
UNWANTED books and toys? What if he'd
disappeared in the dustbin sack that had been
taken to the Organiser?

Jake and Mum looked through every room in
the house together. They came across all sorts
of interesting things! But they didn't find
Wilfred.

Jake was in such a panic that Mum took him to the phone box in his pyjamas.

"I'm sorry," said the Organiser. "The jumble's already been collected and locked in the church hall."

"Don't worry," Mum told Jake. "The jumble sale is tomorrow. We'll be first there."

But Mum and Jake were late. Huge roadworks held up their bus. By the time they reached the hall, it was packed.

"Let's start this end," said Mum. They dived into the crowd.

Jake found himself by a lady selling sweaters and cardigans.

"I'm looking for Wilfred," he said.

"Over there!" boomed Cardigans. She pushed Jake towards an ancient fridge.

"I'm looking for Wilfred," he repeated.

"That's ME!" beamed a man by the fridge. "I'm Electrical."

"But I want my BEAR," said Jake.

"Oh, the BEAR!" said Wilfred. He pointed to a lady with long hair.

Jake squeezed his way across.

"Tickets here!" cried Long Hair. "Buy a ticket here and win this ADORABLE teddy bear."

But the bear in the raffle was bright yellow and brand new. Jake bit his lip.

"What is it, dear?" asked another Helper.

"It's my bear," whispered Jake. "I've lost my bear."

"Speak up," cried the Helper.

"He's got… BLUE TROUSERS," yelled Jake above the din.

"Just a minute." The Helper swooped onto her table.

"Sorry," she announced. "All the blue ones have gone. How about this nice pink pair… with blue flowers?"

Jake took one look and fled.

"WHOOPS!" He crashed into Mum right by the books and toys table. Jake and Mum caught sight of Wilfred at exactly the same moment.

"THAT BEAR!" they cried together and reached forwards.

"Sorry," said Books and Toys. "But that bear is not for sale."

Jake's face fell. Mum drew herself up.

"You see," went on Books and Toys, "it must be a mistake. He was in my jumble bag. But he couldn't possibly be an UNWANTED bear. So I'm saving him… till his Owner turns up."

Jake and Mum both started talking at once.

Books and Toys smiled apologetically. "You do understand," she said, "that with such a SPECIAL bear, I have to be SURE."

Books and Toys bent down and whispered in Jake's ear. She'd taken a good look at Wilfred and asked Jake a question. Only Wilfred's Owner could know the answer.

Jake went pink, but whispered back. Books and Toys chuckled.

"He's your bear, all right," she said. And handed Wilfred over.

Jake didn't let Wilfred out of his sight for the rest of the day. He clutched him extra tightly at bedtime.

"I WISH I knew what you told the Books and Toys lady," said Mum.

Jake went pink again and snuggled down.

"Some things between a Bear and his Owner," he said, "are… PRIVATE!"

"Quite right too," said Mum. And kissed them both goodnight.

The owl who snored

Oliver was a fluffy new owl. And his parents were very proud of him.

But, when he was a few weeks old, Oliver developed a problem. He began to snore!

"AAAAH!" yawned Mr Owl each evening. "I hardly slept a wink."

"AAAAH!" groaned Mrs Owl. "Is that the time already?"

Oliver's parents tried everything.

Oliver slept facing the sun and then with his back to it.

His parents grew so desperate that they took it in turns… to tap Oliver on the beak and to shout: "DON'T SNORE, OLIVER!"

Then one day, when Oliver was making even more noise than usual, an old sheep leaned through the fence.

"Does anyone up there want any wool?" she bleated.

Oliver carried on snoring. But his parents woke with a start.

"For your EARS," explained the sheep.
"That boy of yours sounds just like our
farmer's tractor!"

Oliver's parents blushed. Then they flew down
quietly to collect some wool.

"Take some off my *number*," offered the
sheep. "My coat's thickest there."

Mr and Mrs Owl tugged gently at the wool.
By the time they had finished Oliver was just
waking up.

"Mmmmm," he stretched comfortably on the branch. "What a lovely day's sleep!"

Oliver's parents yawned all night long. They couldn't wait for bedtime.

"Oooooh, twit, twooooh! That tickles!" they giggled, as they stuffed each other's ears.

But the wool didn't work! They could still hear Oliver snoring.

The old sheep shook her head sadly.

"This case is BEYOND ME," she declared. "I'm off... out of earshot."

But not long afterwards the sheep had troubles of her own. She woke up the owls to tell them all about it.

"POOH!" shrieked Mr Owl.

"Dear ME!" squealed Mrs Owl.

"ATISHOO!" sneezed Oliver. "ATISHOO!"

"Dip!" said the old sheep glumly. "Our farmer's just dipped us. It's meant to make us clean and healthy."

"POOH!" cried the owls together. "Is it always that strong?"

The sheep gave a tired smile.

"I went round three times," she said.
"Because no one could read my number!"

Mr and Mrs Owl shuffled uncomfortably on the branch. They began to feel guilty. So they ignored the horrible smell and stayed awake to cheer up the sheep.

They forgot all about Oliver until Mrs Owl felt a gentle pressure against her wing.

"LOOK!" she whispered with great excitement. "Oliver's asleep. And he's… NOT SNORING."

The old sheep drew herself up proudly.

"It must be the dip," she announced. "I can't recommend it for a bath. But at least it's cleared Oliver's nose!"

Our babysitter

Our sitter doesn't say, "Not now",
Or turn the telly low.
Our sitter doesn't groan, "It's late,
So, off to bed you go!"

Our sitter doesn't make us wash,
Or shout, "Clean out the bath!"
Our sitter likes to tell us jokes,
And always makes us laugh.

Our sitter sometimes raids the fridge,
We all join in the snack.
And if it makes our baby burp,
We pat her on the back.

Our sitter rides a motorbike,
He lets us share his gum.
And when our sitter sits with us,
We NEVER miss our mum!